THE FLUFFY
LITTLE CAT

FIRST PUBLISHED IN 2017

THE FLUFFY LITTLE CAT

Story & illustrations by Zoe

All proceeds from the sale of this book
goes directly to Yorkshire Cat Rescue.

One cold, starry night, under the moonlight
sat a young fluffy, and very sad cat.

This cat was beautiful.
But she was all on her own.

Although her tummy felt big and heavy, she felt very hungry.
She wasn't sure why her tummy felt full,
it had been a long time since she had eaten.

1

The fluffy little cat decided to settle down
for the night.

As she closed her eyes she dreamt of a nice warm
house to sleep in with a lovely human that would
look after her & give her tasty food.

She shed a little tear.

3

Suddenly the cat woke
with a fright.

In front of her was a vehicle.
The door opened and a very nice caring voice
asked the little cat if she was OK.

It was clear that the cat was far from OK!
"Oh you poor little thing you need our help!"

Although she was scared the fluffy little cat was happy
to go with this human, especially as it had started to rain.
And her tummy hurt.

5

The nice caring human drove to a house
and a lady came out to meet them.

"This cat needs our help, thank you
for agreeing to take her in at such short notice.
I don't think it will be long until the kittens come.
She needs a nice warm bed and lots of food.
I've decided to name her Gwinny".

The fluffy little cat didnt understand all of the conversation,
but felt happy when she heard the words 'warm & food'.

rescue
lady

8

foster
mummy

Gwinny went inside the warm house with
her new 'foster mummy'. She was given
a big bowl of tasty food and a bowl of fresh
water. She also had a comfy bed to snuggle up in.

Gwinny felt very relieved, she was
feeling a bit strange and her tummy still felt very odd.
But she knew she was safe.

She had a wash and then she curled up in her new bed.

9

HOME
SWEET
HOME

10

Once the morning came, the foster
mummy came downstairs to see how Gwinny
was doing.

She was suprised and delighted to see
not one cat, but three little fluffy faces
all looking up at her.

Gwinny had given birth to two kittens, called Poppy & Jessie.

11

Gwinny loved her babies very much.

They played lots of games together
like chasing toys and rolling around with each other.

Gwinny knew she was very lucky to
be in the foster mummy's house and not outside
in the cold and wet.

However, she did wonder what would happen next
as she knew this home wasn't forever and there were
other cats just like her who needed to be rescued from outside.
Some would also have babies in their tummies that
needed a safe place to be born.

13

14

One day Gwinny's foster mummy explained
that all three of the cats were going
to see the vet.

They would be having a little operation that would make sure
that Gwinny wouldn't have any more kittens.
And her babies would also be having the same operation,
so that they too would never have any kittens.

Gwinny understood that this was important.
After all, she knew that she was very lucky to have her babies in the safe
warm bed at her foster mummy's house.
It could have been very different if she had to have them outside.
It also meant that she never had to worry about Poppy & Jessie being
in the same scary situation that she had found herself in.

And they could all look forward to a new life in their forever homes.

15

Boosters
are ♥♥♥
important

clever
vet →

16

After the little family had all got better from their operations,
it was time for Gwinny to say goodbye to her kittens.
She had looked after them so well.

They were big and strong, and they were
old enough to leave their mummy now.
Gwinny felt very happy because they were going to
a lovely FOREVER home.

They rubbed noses with one another and waved goodbye.

17

18

Now that Gwinny was ready to be re-homed and to find her own humans
the foster mummy took Gwinny to the rescue centre.

At the centre they helped lots of cats
find their new humans and forever homes.

The foster mummy hugged and kissed Gwinny
and said goodbye, they were both sad because they loved each other.

Gwinny felt a bit scared again.
There were lots of other cats at the centre.
She wondered if anyone would notice her.

Yorkshire Cat Rescue

My name is Sooty

My name is Gwinny

20

cat rescue volunteer

foster mummy

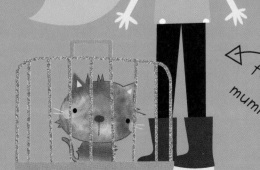

Everyone who worked at the
rescue centre was very nice to all
the cats, and all the kitties had full tummies
and warm heated pads to sleep on.

They had enough room to run around when they
wanted to play. They had somewhere to hide if they were
feeling a bit shy and they had an endless supply of
cat treats and knitted cat nip mice.

But all the cats missed and wanted one thing.
Their very own human and their own home.

One day when it was snowing outside,
Gwinny lay in her bed feeling
sorry for herself. She had been at the
centre for a few months now.

All the staff at the centre could see how beautiful she was.
And they knew she would be chosen one day, but the problem was
the fluffy little cat would hide when people came to see her.

It wasn't her fault, she had forgotten how to smile and show
the people coming to look at her how great she could be.

Just then a man and a lady came up to her pen.

23

As usual, unsure what to do Gwinny hid away.

But the people really wanted to meet her.
They had seen her on the Internet, and wanted to
give her a chance.

They went inside the pen and Gwinny panicked
and tried to escape.
The lady tried to pick her up, but Gwinny forgot
how to be nice and accidently scratched the lady.

She then felt sad, becuase the man and lady looked like
very nice people.

25

Luckily for Gwinny, she was right,
the man and lady were very nice.

They wanted to take her home!

It was still snowing outside, and Gwinny could feel
the cold air within her carry case.

Everyone at the rescue centre came to say
goodbye to Gwinny.

"Oh, she isn't called Gwinny, she is called Tangle
becuase we will enjoy brushing her lovely long fur"
said Tangle's new human lady.

27

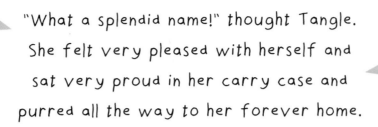

"What a splendid name!" thought Tangle.
She felt very pleased with herself and
sat very proud in her carry case and
purred all the way to her forever home.

When Tangle came through the door,
she looked around and felt excited but a little
bit nervous because everything smelt and looked new.

There was also another cat that already lived there.
He was a big tabby who came from the exact same rescue centre
many years ago.

Perhaps they could be friends?

After hiding behind the televison for a few days,
and once in the cupboard underneath the fish tank,
Tangle decided all this 'being alone' was a bit boring.

One evening when it was quiet and her new
humans were watching television,
she decided to come out and jumped onto the
sofa where her humans were.

The humans smiled, and Tangle settled down.
She allowed her new humans to stroke her head
and before long she was rolling around with her
big fluffy paws up in the air, purring happily
and so proud of herself.

Tangle was finally home.
And this time it was forever.

About Yorkshire Cat Rescue:

Yorkshire Cat Rescue is a small regional rehoming charity which saves the lives of approximately 1000 cats each year.

The charity has a centre at Cross Roads, Keighley, West Yorkshire where the cats are housed prior to adoption.

Yorkshire Cat Rescue neuters, vaccinates and microchips every cat before it goes to its new home.
Other veterinary treatment, along with flea and worm treatment, is given as necessary.

Yorkshire Cat Rescue adopts a positive natural behaviour reinforcement programme which
ultimately finds homes for many "difficult" cats.
No cats are put to sleep other than for welfare reasons on veterinary advice.
Cats which are terminally ill but comfortable are placed in foster homes to enjoy the evening of their lives.

As well as a small salaried team, the charity relies on volunteers and also encourages students who are
studying animal courses to undertake work experience.

The charity relies on fundraising and donations to run, and has a small number of charity shops.

Read about Yorkshire Cat Rescue at https://yorkshirecatrescue.org, or follow Yorkshire Cat Rescue on Facebook.

Yorkshire Cat Rescue - we make unwanted cats wanted.

Tangle's mummy works as a childrenswear designer, and together with her partner Gary, decided to tell
Tangle's story, as it is so common. They decided to aim the book at children to introduce the concept of rescue and
neutering cats to those of a young age (also Tangle's mummy is better at drawing pictures for children)

Printed in Poland
by Amazon Fulfillment
Poland Sp. z o.o., Wrocław